THE LEGEND OF THE STAR

Story by Stacy Gooch-Anderson

Illustrations by Glenn Harmon

ISBN 13: 978-1-59955-243-9

Published by CFI, an imprint of Cedar Fort, Inc.
2373 W. 700 S., Springville, UT 84663
Distributed by Cedar Fort, Inc., www.cedarfort.com

LIBRARY OF CONGRESS CATALOGING-IN-PUBLICATION DATA

Gooch-Anderson, Stacy.
  The legend of the star / Stacy Gooch Anderson.
    p. cm.
  Summary: As all of heaven prepares for the birth of the Savior, a Guardian takes special care of one little cherub, imperfect in body and speech, who wants to participate but seems to have no assigned task. Includes a poem, "The Story of the Star."
  ISBN 978-1-59955-243-9 (acid-free paper)
  [1. Angels--Fiction. 2. Disabilities--Fiction. 3. Trust in God--Fiction. 4. Jesus Christ--Nativity--Fiction. 5. Heaven--Fiction.] I. Gooch-Anderson, Stacy. Story of the star. II. Title.

  PZ.G598Leg 2009
  [E]--dc22

                    2009009052

Jacket and book design by Angela D. Olsen
Edited by Melissa Caldwell
Cover design © 2009 by Lyle Mortimer

Printed on acid-free paper

Printed in Hong Kong

10 9 8 7 6 5 4 3 2 1

Dedication

To everyone who knows of or thinks of themselves
as an "imperfect angel"—May you find your life's mission
so that you too can bless all of us living around you.

"Children, children!" the Cherubus Guardian said, clapping his hands. He motioned the winged youngsters to gather round.

"The time has officially been announced when our Jesus will make his entrance into the world. Each sector of angeldom has been assigned a special task to prepare for His birth."

All of Heaven's cherubs twittered excitedly about having a role in His glorious arrival.

"Will we sing, Guardian?" asked one little cherub. He then puffed out his chest and took a deep breath. He sang a perfectly sweet strain of "Gloria" in seamless harmony with the rest of the Choral Master's gleeful choir. The Cherubus Guardian drew out his hands in a motion for the choir to be silent.

"Yes, some of you will be singing. Others will be playing their trumps," the Guardian said, smiling at another little cherub. The cherub grinned back and quickly breathed on his horn, filling the Cherubic Announcement Hall with its rich sound. He tenderly rubbed the horn with the elbow of his white tunic.

"Jesus will be born in the lowliest of circumstances and be surrounded by our Father's most humble of creatures. Some of you will tame the animals by surrounding them with peace and giving them a view of Heaven on earth." The Guardian chuckled and glanced towards his unkempt little cherubs. They would rather roll in the Heavenly Fields and tumble down the foothills of the Majestic Mountains with puppies and gangly fawns than study scrolls.

"The Seraphs will be spreading good cheer from here all the way to the earth before surrounding His manger. They will radiate His light while the Highest Order of Angelhood visits those awaiting news of His birth," said the Guardian.

"They will also be his guardians when Jesus fulfills His mission on Earth," he said, casting a look of sadness before his charges. "Oh ... but if it could only be different." He reverently wiped a tear from his aged cheek before he began to brighten again.

"And many of you will also be here on the day of His joyful return. Trumps and angels will hail Him through the hallowed halls of Heaven. You, my dear little ones, will be there to not only see Him but to also lift Him to his throne—His seat of rest." The Guardian's eyes once again twinkled at the mere thought of seeing Jesus again.

The guardian then clapped his hands once more and hustled the cherubs off to prepare for the Christ child's birth. That is when he noticed a movement from the corner of his eye. It was he, the only little cherub in Heaven who was imperfect——both in form and in speech. It was beyond any of their understanding as to why he had been created that way. But as is the ways of Heaven's teachings, they drew on their faith that there must be a plan.

The Guardian blushed with shame at his lack of charity during the excitement. He should have had someone pick the little cherub up and assist him into the Announcement Hall. The Guardian rushed to his side before the sweet little angel lost his balance. The Guardian smiled. Sometimes this little one's spirit carried him more exuberantly than his form could manage. No doubt thoughts were formed more clearly behind those eyes than his mumbled speech could ever share. His steadfast spirit was an inspiration to the old Guardian. He spent countless hours protecting this little "broken angel" from the taunting of the more hasty and vigorous youth.

He scooped up the little cherub. His stuttering speech and jerky movements were emphasized by his excitement. He wanted to know what he could do to prepare for the Savior's birth.

The old Guardian's crinkled smile faded when he realized that this little cherub had not been given an assignment. He reassured the little angel and explained that there must have been a mistake. He would call right away the Presiding Quorum's quarters and ask about the oversight. He then carried the little angel to another caregiver and placed him in her outstretched arms. He would look into the matter of the little cherub's special assignment.

"But, sir, his heart is pure even though he body isn't perfect. True, he isn't nimble and his speech is garbled. Is there nothing he can do? Must he watch from afar while all the rest are participating?"

"Cherubus Guardian, I do share your compassion for this little one. I assure you that it is the Father's request that he stay behind. I am sorry," said the Quorum's presiding angel.

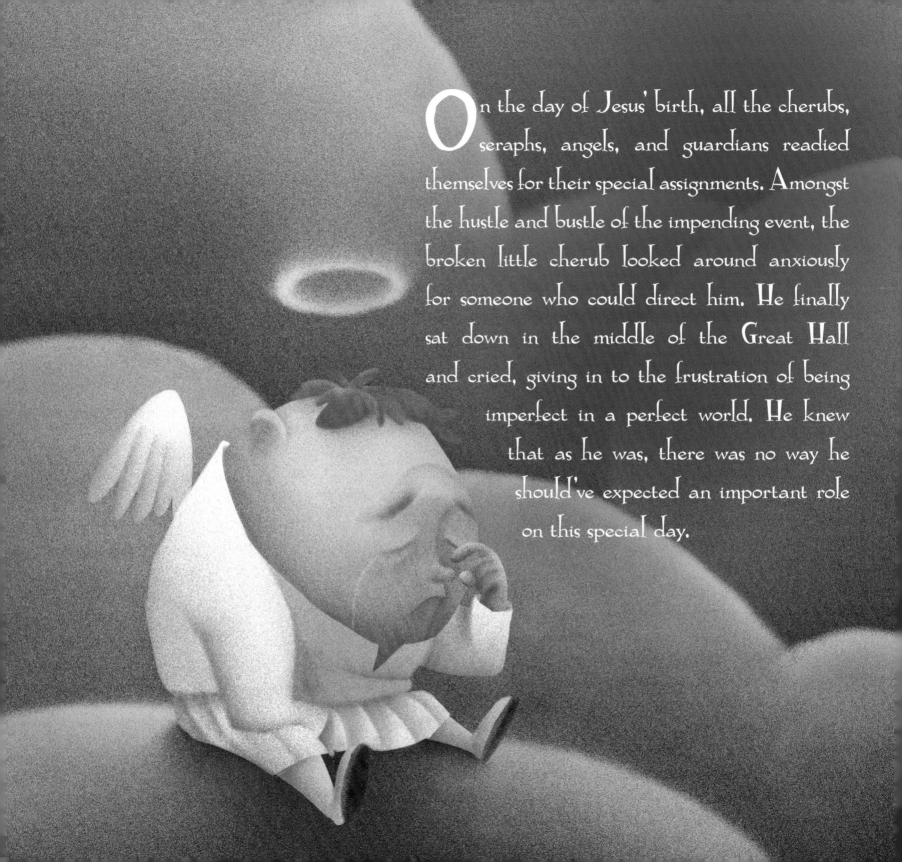

On the day of Jesus' birth, all the cherubs, seraphs, angels, and guardians readied themselves for their special assignments. Amongst the hustle and bustle of the impending event, the broken little cherub looked around anxiously for someone who could direct him. He finally sat down in the middle of the Great Hall and cried, giving in to the frustration of being imperfect in a perfect world. He knew that as he was, there was no way he should've expected an important role on this special day.

The Cherubus Guardian directed the cherubs on preparing for this glorious day. After he had gotten them off to their respective stations, he noticed the broken little cherub, who had glistening tears on his cheeks. In the turmoil of dealing with the little angel's situation and not knowing what to do, the Guardian had finally pushed it to the back of his mind. He had forgotten to consult the matter with his small charge.

He walked over to him and picked him up.

"My little one, do not be discouraged. I am sure Father has a good reason for you to stay behind," he offered, even though he wondered what it could be. He placed the little cherub on his lap and watched the grand event from the Grand Hall's steps. However, he noticed that something was wrong. All was dark and quiet. There were neither joyous strains of "Hallelujah" resonating nor any light to bear good tidings.

As the Cherubus Guardian's thoughts nervously swirled, the broken little cherub's warm tears flowed down his cheeks. When they hit the floor of the Great Hall, they were miraculously transformed into an illuminated path! It roamed out of the window of the Great Hall and fell in a pillar of light to rest upon the Holy Child lying in a manger.

With giant tender droplets still falling from his eyes, the broken little cherub left the secure arms of the Cherubus Guardian. He hobbled to the path of light. With faith, he too roamed out the Great Hall and stumbled into the heavens. And as he did, beneath his feet appeared a most brilliant stepping stone, which carefully carried the little angel. Amongst the music of hallowed harps, voices of the joyful chorus, and the sound of jubilant trumps, the little angel raised his humble voice and sang splendid praises to the newly born babe.

The Cherubus Guardian and all the others standing as Heaven's witnesses watched in awe. With each movement closer to the baby Jesus, the little cherub's deformities were healed, and he became flawless in his Lord's sight. His voice grew stronger, clearer, and more Heavenly than any they'd ever heard before.

A perfect knowledge settled in as finally the wise old Guardian understood the most important lesson any of them had needed to learn. It was for this reason that Jesus had been born——so that those who are broken and troubled, and yet choose to walk towards Him in faith, can also be perfected just as the little cherub had been.

THE STORY OF THE STAR
by Stacy Gooch–Anderson

It's a well known fact that there are five
points upon a star,
But there's a thoughtful message that
goes to this symbol from afar.
Two of these special points spread out
from side to side
Just like the Savior's inviting arms as
with Him we choose to abide.
Two more points touch the ground just
like our Savior's feet
As He walked the earth in service
raising souls from despair and defeat.
The last point ascends towards Heaven
just as Christ did long ago

After giving His life for our sakes so
that more perfected we may grow.
The last thing I need to mention about
this special symbol of comforting light
Is that when connecting the inner points,
there appears an interesting sight.
Another star can be seen within
the progressively smaller pentagons.
One could keep creating forever
just as are the ways of God.
Eternal progression and a Savior's love
are the messages of a star
And these are the lessons taught by this
heavenly symbol from afar.